_____ This book belongs to _____

To Auntie Helen and Auntie Margaret,
two penguins who really are different.

M.O.

To Phillis.

J.N.

ISBN 0-439-31809-2

Text copyright © 2000 by Maria O' Neill.
Illustrations copyright © 2000 by Jill Newton
All rights reserved.
Published by Scholastic Inc., 555 Broadway, New York, NY 10012,
by arrangement with Scholastic Ltd., Commonwealth House.
SCHOLASTIC and associated logos are trademarks and/or
registered trademarks of Scholastic Inc.

12 11 10 9 8 7 6 5 4 3 2 1   1 2 3 4 5 6/0

Printed in China

First American printing, November 2001

The Penguin Who Wanted to Be Different

A Christmas Wish

Maria O'Neill • Jill Newton

SCHOLASTIC INC.

New York   Toronto   London   Auckland   Sydney
Mexico City   New Delhi   Hong Kong   Buenos Aires

Dorothy Penguin followed Uncle Binny up the hill.

"Are we there yet?" asked Dorothy, puffing hard.

"Almost, Dot!" said Uncle Binny, taking Dorothy's hand.

They walked on for a few more minutes and then scrambled up the last big mound of snow. They had reached the top of Glacier Hill.

"Look at that view, Dot!" cried
Uncle Binny. "You can see for miles!"
Dorothy gazed down toward the
village. The houses looked tiny.
And she could see hundreds of penguins
walking around, some playing, some
shopping, some on their way to the park,

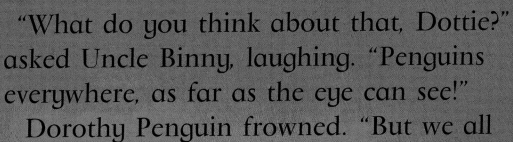

"What do you think about that, Dottie?" asked Uncle Binny, laughing. "Penguins everywhere, as far as the eye can see!"

Dorothy Penguin frowned. "But we all look the same," she said.

The next day, Dorothy wandered into the garden. She was still frowning.

"What's the matter?" asked Dorothy's mother, looking up.

"Mom, I want to be different," said Dorothy. "I'm just the same as all the other penguins and — "

"You are different, Dorothy. You're different and special to me," said Dorothy's mother. "Now, have you written your letter to Santa Claus yet?"
"Not yet, mom, but . . ." Dorothy stammered.

"Why don't you go and see what Uncle Binny is doing?" suggested Dorothy's mom.

Dorothy waddled off sadly.

"Why can't she be like all the other small penguins?" sighed Dorothy's mom as she went back to work.

"Hello, Dottie!" said Uncle Binny. "Have you come to help me fix this old sled?"

"Uncle Binny, how can I make myself different?" Dorothy asked eagerly.

"What a strange question," replied Uncle Binny, kindly. "Why would you want to be different when you're lucky enough to be a penguin?"

"But Uncle Binny — " said Dorothy.

"Don't be silly, Dottie!" interrupted
Uncle Binny. "Now, what are you going
to ask Santa to bring you for Christmas?"

"I don't know yet," Dorothy mumbled,
kicking up the snow. "I'm going out to
play. See you later." Dorothy slid off.
She liked sliding on the ice.

Dorothy's twin friends, Ness and Rory,
were playing outside their house.
"Hello, Dot!" giggled Ness.
"Look at our list of presents," said Rory.
"We asked for a sled, two new scarves,
and a snow wars computer game!"

"And here's our letter to Santa," cried Ness excitedly. "Have you written your letter yet?"

"Not yet," said Dorothy thoughtfully. "But maybe I should."

She borrowed a piece of paper from the twins and began to write very carefully.

Here is Dorothy's letter:

Dear Santa,
   I'm sorry to bother you right now when you're so busy, but I would like a very special present this year.
   I want to be DIFFERENT!
   That would be the best present of all. I know you can do it, Santa. Thank you very much.
                    Love,
                    Dorothy XOXO
   P.S. I've been very good this year. Ask Mom.

Dorothy felt very pleased with herself. She mailed the letter to Santa and skipped off to play.

On Christmas Eve, Dorothy's mother tucked her into bed.

"Good night, Dorothy. Sleep well."
"Good night, Mom," said Dorothy happily. "I can't wait until tomorrow."
Dorothy's mother smiled.

In the middle of the night, an old man with a bushy white beard and sparkling eyes called to his friends.

"It's time, everyone," he said. "We have to start work. Hurry!"

A small elf whispered into his ear.

"What's that?" asked Santa. "Two elves
are in bed with the flu, and one of the
reindeer has twisted his ankle? But it's
our busiest night of the year," he sighed.
"What shall we do?"

Suddenly, he remembered a very
special letter that he had stuffed into
his pocket earlier.

Dorothy was fast asleep and dreaming, when she felt a gentle touch on her shoulder.

"We need your help," said a voice. "There are so many children to visit and so many presents to deliver . . ."

"Of course, I'll help," Dorothy beamed.
She was so excited she nearly fell over. Out
of all the penguins in the world, Santa had
chosen her to help.

All night long, Santa, Dorothy, the elves, and the reindeer flew all over the world delivering presents.

Until at last they were almost home.

"This is the last one, Dorothy," said
Santa sleepily. "Thanks for all your help."

Dorothy carefully put the last present under the village Christmas tree and turned toward home.

She quietly climbed back into bed and was asleep in no time at all. The sleigh whizzed away into the darkness.

Early on Christmas morning, Uncle Binny arrived. "Merry Christmas! Merry Christmas!" he boomed. "Where's Dottie? Come on, let's go!"

Dorothy, Mom, and Uncle Binny went
out to see the big Christmas tree
in the village.

All the small penguins were squealing
with excitement and unwrapping lots
of presents.

"Look at my wonderful new sled!"
shrieked Ness.
"Look at my new snow goggles!"
shrieked Rory.
There was one very small present
left under the tree.

"This one's for you, Dottie,"
said Uncle Binny. "It's from Santa."
Dorothy read Santa's note:

To Dorothy, a very special penguin.
See you next year! Love, Santa

She slowly unwrapped the small present.

"Is that all you got?" Ness shouted, zooming past. Dorothy proudly put on her new elf hat.

"It's just what I wanted," she beamed.

Now, at last, although she looked just the same, Dorothy Penguin felt a little bit different.